PUFFIN BOOKS

Clickety clack!

Who's
coming
down
the
track?

It's Babysitter Bear!

Babysitter Bear is looking after me, because today is a VERY IMPORTANT DAY in our house.

"It certainly is!" says Babysitter Bear.

"Your mummy and daddy will be very busy."

"You can be my big helper," says Babysitter Bear.
"First we'll collect all the babies.
Where shall we take them today?"

To Picnic Park,
of course!

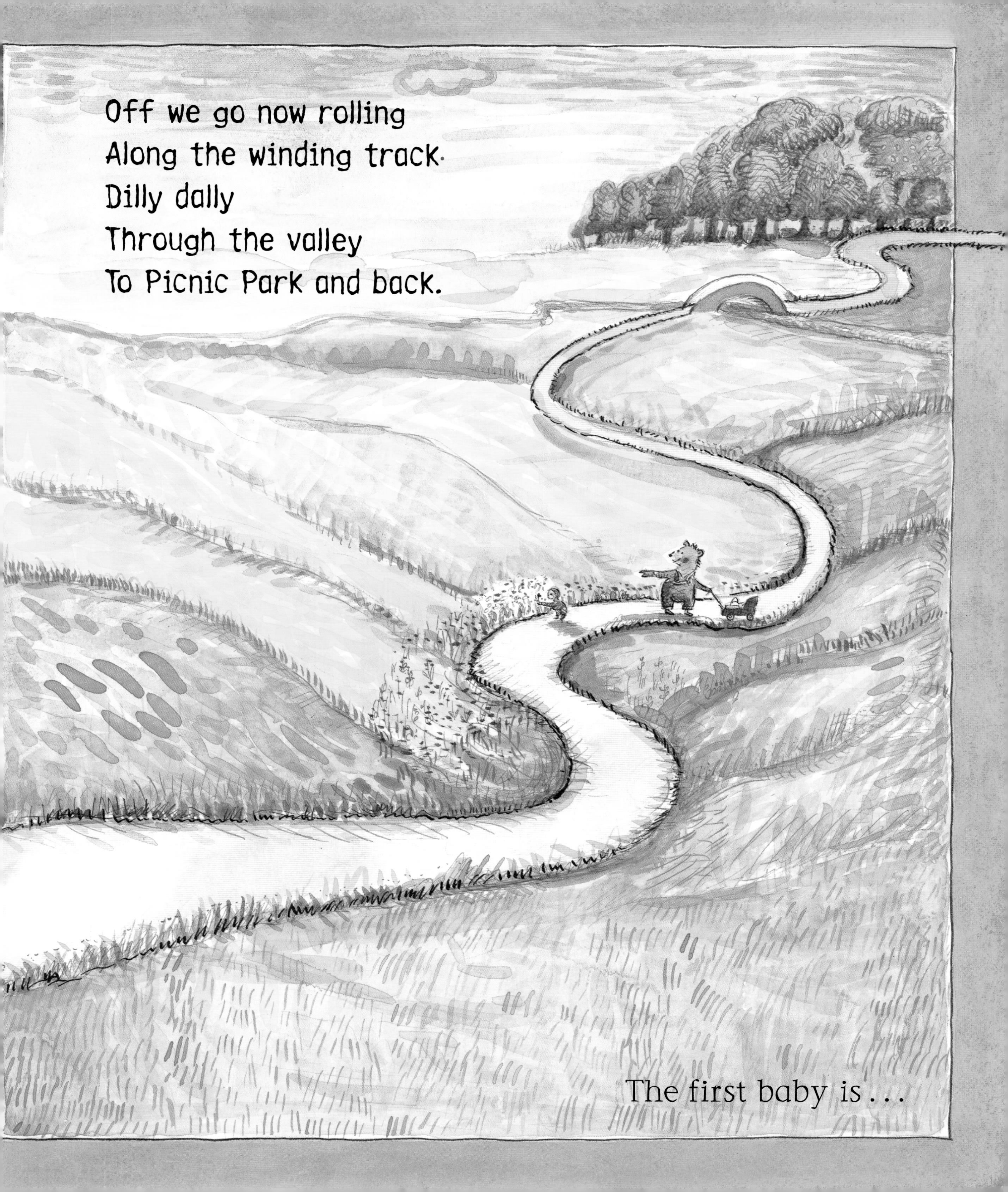

Off we go now rolling
Along the winding track.
Dilly dally
Through the valley
To Picnic Park and back.

The first baby is . . .

"He likes his
hair brushed
at twelve,

a story
at one,

a cuddle
at two

and don't
forget his
blanket."

One bouncy baby rolling
Along the winding track
Where the breeze
Blows through the trees
To Picnic Park and back.

The next baby is . . .

. . . Roly Rabbit.

"She likes a
crawl at ten,

a tickle
at eleven,

a bounce
at twelve

and she must
wear a strap
in the buggy."

Two bouncy babies rolling
Along the winding track
Where the flowers
Are tall as towers
To Picnic Park and back.

The next baby is . . .

. . . Podgy Piglet.

"He likes his breakfast
at nine, a snack at ten,
elevenses at eleven,
lunch at twelve,
pudding at one and
a little something
in between."

Three bouncy babies rolling
Along the winding track
Where the waves
Crash through the caves
To Picnic Park and back.

The next babies are . . .

. . . the Sleepy Seals.

"They like their snooze in the morning,

a nap at lunchtime,

forty winks at four

and a rest before bedtime."

Five bouncy babies rolling
Along the winding track
On we go
Through the snow
To Picnic Park and back.

The next baby is . . .

. . . Stinky Skunk.

"He likes
his nappy
at nine,

his potty
at ten,

wee-wees
at eleven

and I think
he needs
changing now."

Six bouncy babies rolling
Along the winding track
There's the swing
And EVERYTHING
It's lovely to be back.

It's always playtime with Babysitter Bear.

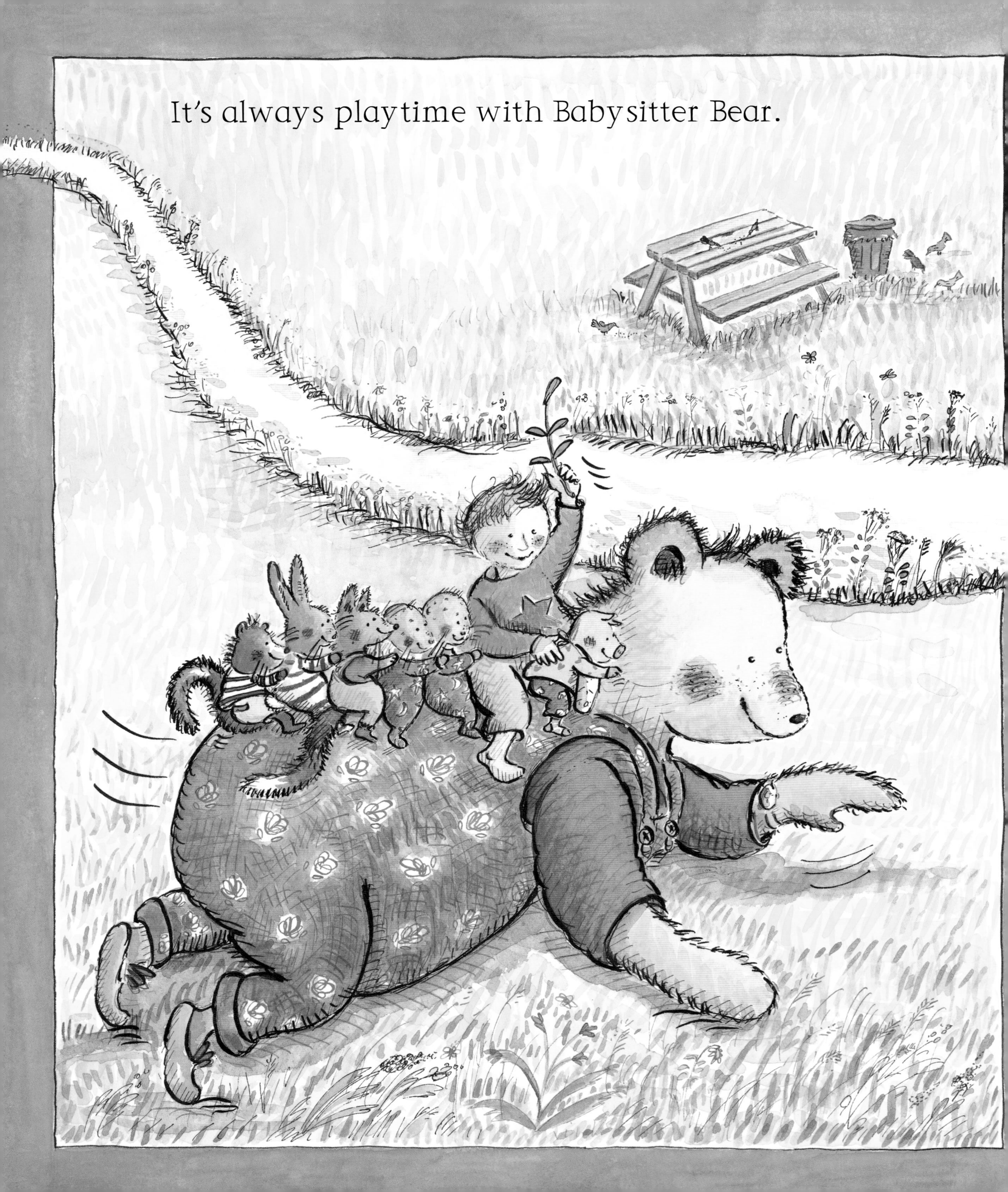

"Let's have our picnic," says Babysitter Bear. "What hungry babies! Don't worry, Podgy Piglet, there's plenty for everyone!"

"Phew, it's hard work
looking after babies,"
says Babysitter Bear. "I'll
just sit down for a moment."

Stop that buggy rolling
Flying down the track
Shooting past
Way too fast
Through Picnic Park and...

...SPLAT!

Poor old Babysitter Bear!
But don't worry,

I'll give Fluffy Fox his blanket

and Podgy Piglet his pudding . . .

. . . and Roly Rabbit a tickle.

I'll wake up the Seals, otherwise they won't sleep tonight.

But I'm leaving Stinky Skunk for you.

"Whatever would I do without my big helper?" says Babysitter Bear.

Six sleepy babies rolling
Along the winding track
It's nearly dark
In Picnic Park
Let's take the babies back.

Goodnight, Stinky Skunk.
Goodnight, Sleepy Seals.
Goodnight, Podgy Piglet.
Goodnight, Roly Rabbit.
Goodnight, Fluffy Fox.
Phew! It's hard work looking after babies.

One BIG baby rolling
Along the winding track
Going home
On our own
Now we're nearly back.

Did you remember, Babysitter Bear, today
is a VERY IMPORTANT DAY in our house?

"It certainly is!" says Babysitter Bear.
"Look, here's your mummy . . .
she's holding something very carefully.
I think I know what it is."

The last baby is . . .

. . . OUR VERY OWN BRAND NEW BABY!
As fluffy as a fox,
as roly as a rabbit,
as podgy as a piglet,
as sleepy as a seal
and just a tiny bit pongy!

Goodnight,
Babysitter Bear!

Off she goes now rolling
Along the winding track
Beneath the moon
Please take us soon
To Picnic Park . . .

. . . and back!